# An Old-Fashioned
# THANKSGIVING

ISBN-13: 978-0-8249-5620-2

Published by Ideals Children's Books
An imprint of Ideals Publications
A Guideposts Company
Nashville, Tennessee
www.idealsbooks.com

Color separations by Precision Color Graphics, Franklin, Wisconsin

Printed and bound in China

Library of Congress CIP data on file

Designed by Eve DeGrie

Leo_Jun10_1


The publisher would like to thank the Williamsburg, Virginia, Regional
Library; Rod and Jody Wheeler; and Julie Brooks for the loan of the artwork
featured on pages 13, 34, and 36.

 For the Wheeler sisters, Margaret, Jane, and Betty ~J.W.

# An Old-Fashioned
# THANKSGIVING

Written by LOUISA MAY ALCOTT

Illustrated by JODY WHEELER

ideals children's books.
Nashville, Tennessee

**M**any years ago, up among the New Hampshire hills, Farmer Bassett lived with his wife and a houseful of sturdy sons and daughters. They were poor in money, but rich in land and love. Their old farmhouse was a very happy home.

Now, November had come and the crops were in. In the fireplace a cheerful fire roared, and savory smells were in the air. Down among the red embers, saucepans simmered, suggestive of an approaching feast.

A baby lay in the cradle, two small boys sat shelling corn for popping and sorting hazelnuts, and four young girls stood at the long table, busily chopping meat, pounding spice, and slicing apples. Farmer Bassett and Eph, the oldest boy, were doing chores outside, for

Thanksgiving was at hand and all must be in order for that time-honored day. To and fro, from table to hearth, bustled Mrs. Bassett, all flushed and floury.

Tilly, the eldest daughter, said, "I think it's real fun to have Thanksgiving at home. But I'm sorry that Gran'ma is sick, and we can't go there as usual."

"Here's a man comin' up the hill lively! Guess it's
Gad Hopkins. Pa told him to bring a dozen oranges if
they weren't too high!" shouted Sol and Seth, running
to the door.

But all were disappointed, for it was not Gad with
the much-desired fruit. It was a stranger, who hurried
up to Mr. Bassett with some brief message that made
the farmer drop his ax.

The man said old Mr. Chadwick
told him to tell Mrs. Bassett her
mother was failin' fast, and she'd
better come today.

The children helped their mother get ready, and by the time the sleigh was at the door, Mrs. Bassett was waiting with the baby done up in blankets.

"Now, Eph, you must keep up the fires, for there's a storm brewin'," said Mr. Bassett.

"Tilly, put extra comfortables on the beds," said Mrs. Bassett. "Pa will come back tomorrow night. Keep snug and be good."

"Yes'm, goodbye!" called the children, as Mrs. Bassett was driven away, leaving a stream of directions behind her.

Eph put on his biggest boots and surveyed his responsibilities. Tilly began to order about the younger girls. They soon forgot Granny and found it great fun to keep house all alone.

The few flakes soon increased to a regular snowstorm; for up among the hills, winter came early and lingered long. But Tilly got them a good dinner, and Eph kept up a glorious fire.

When the clock struck nine, Tilly tucked up the children and, having kissed them all around as Mother did, she crept into her own nest.

When they woke, it was still snowing. After a brisk scrub, the
little Bassetts went downstairs with cheeks glowing like apples.

"Now about dinner," began Tilly.

"Ma didn't expect us to have a real Thanksgiving dinner,"
interrupted Prue, doubtfully.

"I can roast a turkey and make a pudding as well as anybody,

I guess," cried Tilly. "Pa is coming tonight, so we won't have dinner till late. That will give us plenty of time."

"Did you ever roast a turkey?" asked Roxy with interest.

"Should you try?" said Rhody, in an awestruck tone.

"You will see what I can do. All you have to do is let me work," commanded Tilly.

So Tilly attacked the plum pudding. She had seen her mother do it many times. But she forgot both sugar and salt, and she tied the preparation so tightly in the cloth that it had no room to swell. Happily unconscious of these mistakes, Tilly popped it into a pot of boiling water.

"I can't remember the flavorin'," Tilly said as she soaked her bread for the stuffing. "Seems to me it's sweet marjoram or summer savory, so let's put in both. The best herbs are in the attic—you get some, Prue," commanded Tilly, diving into the mess.

Prue set aside her onion-chopping and trotted to the dark attic. But with a nose that smelled only onions, she got catnip and wormwood instead. Eager to be of use, she pounded up the herbs and scattered them into the large bowl.

"It doesn't smell just right, but I suppose it will when it is cooked," said Tilly as she filled the empty turkey. Then, she set it by till its hour came.

It took a long time to get the vegetables ready, for the girls thought they would have every sort. Eph helped, and by noon all was ready for cooking.

"Now you all go out and sled while Prue and I set the table," said Tilly, bent on having her dinner look good.

Out came the rough sleds and away trudged the four younger Bassetts to amuse themselves in the snow.

Eph played his fiddle in the parlor while the girls set the table. The cloth was coarse, but white as snow. They had no napkins and little silver; but the best tankard and Ma's few wedding spoons were set forth in state. The place of honor was left in the middle for the oranges yet to come.

"Doesn't it look beautiful?" said Prue.

"I wish Ma could see it," began Tilly, when a loud howling sent both girls flying to the window.

In the twilight, they saw four small figures tearing up the road to come bursting in, all screaming at once, "The bear, the bear! Eph, get the gun!"

"Down in the holler, sleddin', we heard a growl," began Sol.

"I saw him first, lookin' over the wall," roared Seth.

"Aw-f-ful big and sh-shaggy," quavered Roxy.

Rhody piped out, "I was so scared my legs would hardly go."

"We ran as fast as we could, and he came growling after us. He's awful hungry," added Sol.

"Eph, don't let him eat us," cried both little girls, flying upstairs to hide under their mother's bed.

"No danger of that. I'll shoot him as soon as he comes." Eph said as he raised the window.

"Don't miss!" cried Seth, following Sol, who had climbed to the top of the cupboard.

Prue stationed herself by the hearth. But Tilly boldly stood at the open window.

"Get the ax, Tilly, and if I miss, keep him off while I load again," said Eph.

Tilly flew for the ax and was at her brother's side by the time the bear was near.

"Fire, Eph!" cried Tilly firmly.

"Wait till he rears again. I'll get a better shot," answered the boy.

Suddenly, Tilly threw down the ax, flung open the door, and ran straight into the arms of the bear, who stood up straight to receive her. The growlings changed to a loud "Haw, haw!"

"It's Gad Hopkins tryin' to fool us!" cried Eph.

"Gad! How could you scare us so!" laughed Tilly.

Gad drew a dozen oranges from some deep pocket and fired them into the window with such good aim that Eph ducked, Prue screamed, and Sol and Seth came down much quicker than they went up.

"Well, I upset my sleigh, and the horse left me, so I tied on my buffalo skins and walked till I saw the children sleddin'. I just meant to give 'em a little scare, but when they ran, I kept up the joke," roared Gad, haw-hawing again.

"Come in and have dinner with us," cried Tilly. "Pa will be along soon, I reckon."

"I can't. My folks will think I'm dead if I don't get along home," said Gad, taking a kiss from Tilly's rosy cheek. His cheek tingled with the smart slap she gave him as she ran away.

"Sakes alive—the turkey is burnt on one side!" scolded Tilly.

"Well, I couldn't think of dinner when I expected to be eaten alive," said Prue, who had tumbled into the cradle when the rain of oranges began.

Tilly laughed and all the rest joined in. The older girls dished up the dinner and were struggling to get the pudding out of the cloth when Roxy called out, "Here's Pa!"

"There's folks with him," added Rhody.

"Lots of 'em! I see two big sleighs chock-full," shouted Seth.

"It looks like a funeral. Guess Gran'ma's dead and come up to be buried here," said Sol solemnly.

"If that's a funeral, the mourners are uncommonly jolly," said Eph, as merry voices broke the white silence without.

"I see Aunt Cinthy, and Cousin Hetty—and there's Moses and Amos," cried Prue.

"Oh, I'm so glad I got dinner!" cried Tilly.

"Isn't Gran'ma dead at all?" asked Sol, as in poured Father, Mother, Baby, aunts, and cousins.

"Bless your heart, no!" answered Ma. "It was all a mistake. Mother was sittin' up as chipper as you please, and dreadful sorry you didn't all come."

"So, to give you a taste of the fun, your Pa fetched us all up to spend the evenin'," said Aunt Cinthy.

"What in the world set you to gettin' up such a supper?" asked Mr. Bassett, looking about him.

Tilly modestly began to tell, but the others broke in and sang her praises in a sort of chorus, in which bears, pies, and oranges were oddly mixed. Tilly and Prue served dinner, sure everything was perfect.

But when big Cousin Moses took the first taste of the stuffing, he nearly choked.

"Tilly Bassett," demanded Ma, for all the rest were laughing, "whatever made you put wormwood and catnip in your stuffin'?"

"I did it," said Prue, nobly taking all the blame, which caused Pa to kiss her on the spot and declare that it didn't do a mite of harm, for the turkey was all right.

"Well, I've never seen onions cooked better," said Aunt Cinthy. "The dinner is a credit to you, my dears."

The pudding was an utter failure. It was speedily whisked out of sight, and all fell upon the pies, which were perfect.

"Blindman's buff" and other lively games soon set everyone
bubbling over with merriment. And when Eph struck up his
fiddle, old and young fell into their places for a dance.
Apples and cider and singing finished the evening, and
after a grand kissing all around, the guests
drove off in the clear moonlight, which
came just in time to cheer
their long drive.

When the jingle of the last bell had died away, Mr. Bassett said soberly as they stood together on the hearth: "Children, we have special cause to be thankful that the sorrow we expected was changed into joy. So we'll read a chapter before we go to bed and give thanks where thanks are due."

Then Tilly set out the light stand with the big Bible on it and a candle on each side, and all sat quietly in the firelight, smiling as they listened with happy hearts to the sweet old words that fit all times and seasons so beautifully.

When the "good nights" were over and the children in bed, Prue put her arm around Tilly, for she was sure she was crying.

"Don't mind about the old stuffin' and puddin'," Prue whispered tenderly. "Ma said we really did do surprisin' well for such young girls."

Tilly broke out into laughter and Prue could not help

joining her, even before she knew the cause of the merriment.

"I'm laughing to think how Gad fooled Eph. I thought Moses and Amos would have died over it when I told them, it was so funny," explained Tilly when she got her breath.

"I was so scared that when the first orange hit me, I thought it was a bullet and scrabbled into the cradle as fast as I could," laughed Prue, as Tilly gave a growl.

A smart rap on the wall of the next room caused a sudden lull in the fun, and Mrs. Bassett's voice was heard, saying, "Girls, go to sleep or you'll wake the baby."

"Yes'm," answered two meek voices, and after a few giggles, silence reigned, broken only by an occasional snore from the boys or the soft scurry of mice in the buttery, taking their part in this old-fashioned Thanksgiving.